Chocolate Socks

Written by Holly Durst

Illustrated by Brandon Fall

Ambassador International

GREENVILLE, SOUTH CAROLINA & BELFAST, NORTHERN IRELAND

www.ambassador-international.com

CHOCOLATE SOCKS

Printed in the United States of America

ISBN: 978-1-62020-000-1
eISBN: 978-1-62020-016-2

Cover and Inside art by Brandon Fall
Author photo by Jennie Raff

AMBASSADOR INTERNATIONAL
Emerald House
427 Wade Hampton Blvd.
Greenville, SC 29609, USA
www.ambassador-international.com

AMBASSADOR BOOKS
The Mount
2 Woodstock Link
Belfast, BT6 8DD, Northern Ireland, UK
www.ambassador-international.com

The colophon is a trademark of Ambassador

DEDICATION FOR CHOCOLATE SOCKS

To all my friends and family who encouraged me to turn this dream into a reality. I am blessed to know each and every one of you. Many thanks and all my love!

—Holly

If I could have **anything,** what would it be?
Not something from **Santa** or the **Easter Bunny.**

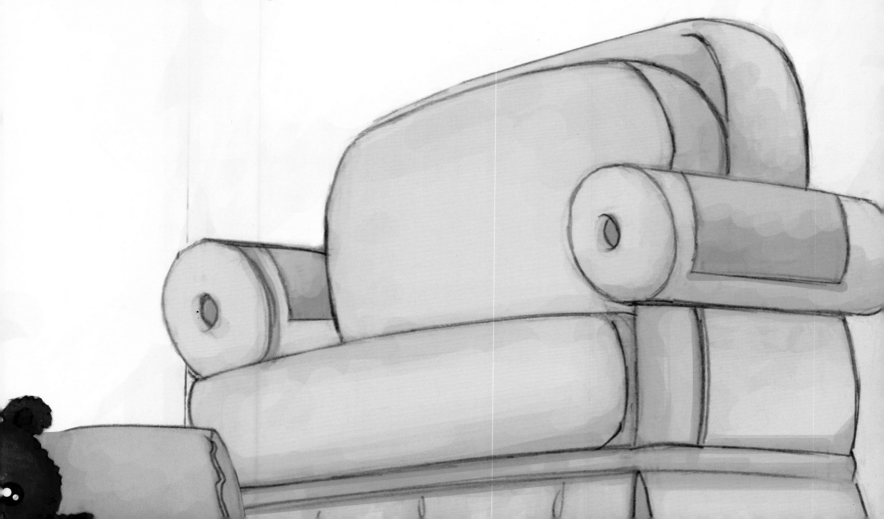

What I want is simple yet strange

You can't even buy it with all your loose change.

My two favorite things, made into one
Socks made of chocolate, oh how fun!

I know what you are thinking,
how weird can this be

For me to want something so silly, you see

But this is my dream
to have chocolate socks
All wrapped up,
with a bow and a box

If I can have them, I promise to share

Every boy and girl
shall receive a pair

And who wouldn't want these socks on their feet

Always warm and toasty and yet a very yummy treat

But take my advice
and keep them indoors
You wouldn't want chocolate
all over the floors

Who is with me on this?
I think it sounds great!
Its always fun to think
and create.

So, what are your two favorite things?
Think about it and follow your dreams

GRAND OPENING

Never give up on what you do
Because my dream of chocolate socks
finally came true!

Holly Durst was born and raised in a small town in Ohio. She graduated with a Bachelors degree in Communication from Walsh University. Holly then moved to Los Angeles where she discovered her love for writing childrens books. Her two favorite things are chocolate and socks. The idea for writing her first book came when Holly was given a gift of a box of chocolate and a pack of socks. The idea is priceless!

While living in Los Angeles, Holly managed a high end clothing boutique in Beverly Hills for five years. It was there, where she was spotted and asked to be on ABC's hit show 'The Bachelor.' Three years after her unsuccessful quest for love on television, Holly was asked to come back for season two of 'Bachelor Pad.' This venture was a lot more successful than the last.

Bachelor Pad is a competition show competing for love and money. On the show she met Blake Julian, a previous contestant on 'The Bachelorette.' They started dating after the show and by the finale, they were engaged. The engagement wasn't the only big thing to happen to Holly on the show; she won! Holly walked away with $125,000 and the love of her life!

Holly currently resides in Greenville, South Carolina. Blake has a dental practice there, Signature Smiles, so she happily moved across the country to be with him. Holly gives all her praise to God for His many blessings in her life.

For more information about
Holly Durst
&
CHOCOLATE SOCKS
please visit:

www.hollydurst.com
ChocSox@gmail.com
@HollyDurst
www.facebook.com/HollyDurst

For more information about
AMBASSADOR INTERNATIONAL
please visit:

www.ambassador-international.com
@AmbassadorIntl
www.facebook.com/AmbassadorIntl